ILLUSTRATED CLASSICS

PETER PAN

J. M. BARRIE

ADAPTED BY ANNE ROONEY · ILLUSTRATED BY ROBERT DUNN

Sandy Creek
NEW YORK

The Darling Family

All children, except one, grow up. Wendy discovered she would grow up when she was two. She picked a flower and took it to her mother, who said, "Oh, why can't you remain like this forever?"

So Wendy knew that she would one day grow up.

Mrs. Darling had been married in a white dress and looked truly lovely. Soon, Wendy came along. At first, Mr. Darling was not sure they could afford to have a child. He fussed about the cost, even saying he was not sure they could keep her. But they did keep her, of course, and John and Michael when they came along.

In those days, everyone had a nanny. The Darlings had one too, but because they were poor, their nanny was a large Newfoundland dog called Nana. She was an extremely good nanny, excellent at bath-time and waking at night whenever the children needed her—her kennel was in the nursery where they slept. Although no one could fault Nana, Mr. Darling worried what people would say—no one else employed a dog as a nanny.

The family was untroubled, except that Mrs. Darling wondered about a person named Peter Pan that Wendy mentioned occasionally. She half-remembered believing stories about such a boy when she was small—a boy who lived with the fairies, somewhere called Neverland. But even if he existed then, she thought, he must be grown up by now. Mr. Darling said, "It's nonsense. It will blow over."

But it did not blow over. One morning, Mrs. Darling found dead leaves on the nursery floor.

"Peter must have let them in," Wendy said. "He flies through the window at night sometimes."

Mrs. Darling thought Wendy was dreaming. But she had seen the leaves herself. The next night, Mrs. Darling fell asleep watching over the children. She was woken by a bright light flittering around. A boy stood before her. He was dressed in the skeletons of leaves, and still had all his baby teeth. She knew instantly who it was.

Seeing a grown-up, Peter gnashed his tiny teeth. Nana leaped to slam the window as he escaped, but his shadow was caught and snapped clean off. It hung limply from the window looking messy, so Mrs. Darling folded it neatly away in a drawer.

On Friday, Mr. and Mrs. Darling were going out. They went to say goodnight to the children and told Michael to take his medicine. He refused.

"My medicine tastes worse," Mr. Darling said.

Michael said he would take his medicine if Father took his, too. But Mr. Darling slipped his medicine into Nana's milk. Nana didn't like that at all. Mr. Darling became angry—it had only been a joke. Although he knew it wasn't fair on Nana, he shut her outside. And that is how it all began: without Nana, there was no one in the nursery with the children. A sparkling light in the night sky called out, "Now, Peter!"

The night lights in the nursery went out, but another light twinkled a thousand times brighter. It flitted from drawers to closets, hunting for Peter's shadow.

"Tinkerbell, where's my shadow?" asked Peter, slipping through the window.

They found it in the drawer. Peter hoped it would attach by itself, and then tried to stick it on with soap. Finally, he sat on the floor and cried. Wendy awoke.

"Boy, why are you crying?" she asked.

"What's your name?" he said.

"Wendy Moira Angela Darling. What's yours?" But she knew before he answered. Peter explained that he couldn't make his shadow stick.

"I'll sew it on for you," Wendy said. She stitched it to Peter's foot so securely that it stayed stuck.

"Oh, I am clever!" Peter crowed. Wendy became quite angry, because she was the one who had been clever.

"How old are you?" Wendy asked.

"I don't know," Peter said. "Quite young. I ran away the day I was born. I heard Mother and Father talk about me growing up. I never want to grow up, so I ran away to Kensington Gardens to live with the fairies."

He told her all about fairies—how they are born from babies' laughter and that each time a child says, "I don't believe in fairies," one dies. It suddenly struck Peter that Tinkerbell was keeping very quiet. The little fairy had been shut in the drawer and was furious!

Off to Neverland

Wendy was delighted with Tinkerbell and wished she could be her fairy. Tinkerbell made a sound like tinkling bells, which is how fairy language sounds.

"She is not very polite," Peter said. "She says you are a big, ugly girl and she is my fairy."

"Where do you live now?" Wendy asked.

"In Neverland," Peter Pan said, "with the lost boys. I am captain. But we are lonely because there are no girls. You must come to Neverland and look after us!"

He began to drag her to the window.

"Let go!" Wendy cried, trying to shake him off.

"We'll fly there. I can teach you," he pleaded.

Wendy was unsure.

"You can fly through the stars and see mermaids," he promised, "and tell us stories and tuck us in each night."

"Could John and Michael come, too?" Wendy asked.

Peter agreed that they could. Wendy woke them, and without a thought for their poor parents, Peter Pan sprinkled them with fairy dust and taught them to fly.

As Mr. and Mrs. Darling walked home, they looked up and saw four figures flying around near the nursery ceiling. Mr. Darling rushed to the room, but it was too late. Peter led the three children out through the window. Mr. and Mrs. Darling and Nana would blame themselves for a long time for arriving too late and not being more careful.

Flight and Fight

"Second star to the right and straight on till morning," Peter said was the way to Neverland. They flew on and on. Sometimes it was dark and sometimes light. Often they were tired and cold. When they were hungry, they stole food from the beaks of passing birds.

At last, the island came into view. The children recognized it immediately because they had visited in their imaginations many times. They were thrilled to see the lagoon and the Indians. They flew over a pirate asleep in the grass. Peter explained there were lots of pirates on the island, and their captain was James Hook.

"Is he big?" John asked.

"He's not as big as he was," Peter said, "because I cut off his right hand. Now he has an iron hook instead. Promise that if you meet him in a fight, you will leave him to me." John promised.

Tinkerbell flew alongside. She said the pirates had seen them and prepared their guns. Tink's twinkling light made them an easy target, so Peter took John's hat and dropped her into it. A terrifying roar shattered the night sky. Suddenly, the difference between an imagined island and a real island with pirates was horribly obvious.

Wendy called out to the others but heard only mocking echoes. Tinkerbell said, "Follow me," but, filled with jealousy and hatred for the girl Peter liked, the fairy led Wendy toward her doom.

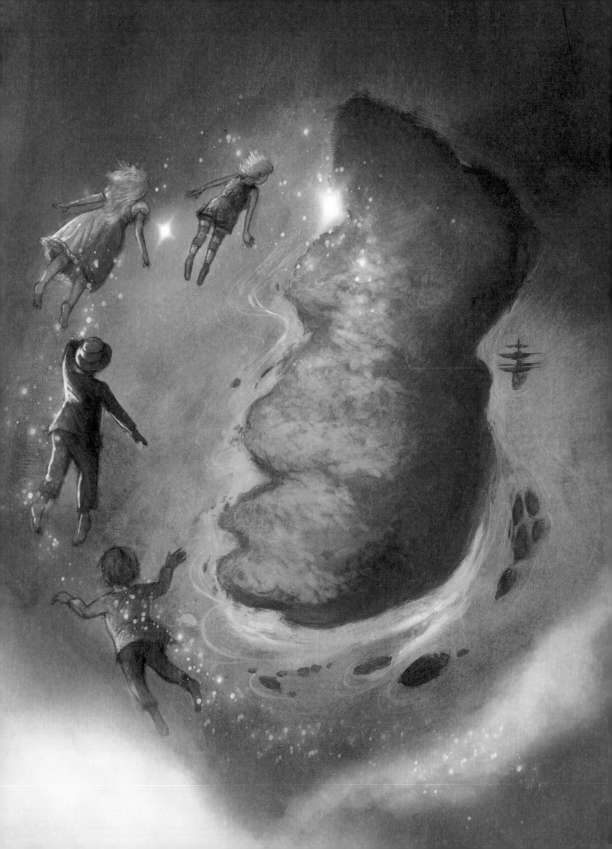

The island always livened up when Peter returned. The lost boys were out looking for Peter, the pirates were looking for the lost boys, the Indians were looking for the pirates, and the beasts were looking for the Indians. They all went around and around the island in a great circle.

There were six lost boys: Tootles, Nibs, Slightly, Curly, and the twins. They dressed in the skins of bears they had killed themselves. Next came the pirates, too many to list. In the middle of the gang, Hook lay on a chariot pulled by his men. He was handsome, with eyes as blue as a forget-me-not and long dark curls. His iron hook gleamed. After the pirates came the Indians, the Piccaninny tribe, walking silently even over broken twigs, with the lovely but haughty princess Tiger Lily at the rear. Finally, the wild beasts followed. Tigers, lions, bears, and many other kind lived on the island. Last of all came the crocodile. We will soon see who she is looking for.

"Yo ho, yo ho, the pirate life,
The flag o' skull and bones,
A merry hour, a hempen rope,
And hey for Davy Jones."

At the sound of the pirate song, the lost boys disappeared in a flash to their underground home. Puzzled, Hook sat down. But then he jumped up again.

"Smee, this mushroom is hot!" he said. And it was—he had discovered the chimney of the lost boys' home.

The pirates were all for fighting, but Hook had a plan.

"We'll make a rich cake and leave it by the shore. They will die, not knowing how dangerous it is to eat rich, wet cake." But just then, an approaching noise froze Hook's blood: tick tick tick tick . . .

"The crocodile," he whispered. When Peter had cut off Hook's hand, he had thrown it to the crocodile. The crocodile liked it so much she had searched for the rest of Hook ever since. Luckily for Hook, the crocodile had swallowed a clock, too, so he could hear her approaching. With the pirates distracted, the lost boys came out again. Nibs looked up to the sky.

"A great white bird is flying this way, calling, 'Poor Wendy!'" he cried. Slightly pretended he had heard of a type of bird called "Wendies."

"Peter says you must shoot the Wendy," Tinkerbell called down.

Always obedient to Peter, the boys took their bows and arrows. Wendy fell to the ground, Tootles's arrow through her chest. The boys gathered around her.

"This is no bird," Slightly said. "I think it was a lady."

"And we have killed her!" Nibs said.

A moment later, they heard Peter crow.

"I have brought you a mother!" he said with delight as he landed. They crowded around, hiding Wendy.

"Why don't you cheer?" Peter asked. So Tootles showed him the terrible truth.

Making a House

"Whose arrow is this?" Peter asked, lifting it from Wendy's chest.

"Mine," Tootles said. Peter raised his hand to stab Tootles with the arrow, but his hand wouldn't move. Wendy had a hold of it!

"She lives!" Peter said. The arrow had struck a button on a chain around her neck. When the boys told Peter that Tinkerbell said he wanted them to kill Wendy, Peter banished her for a week. Tinkerbell had never wanted to pinch Wendy as much as she did just then.

The lost boys were afraid to move Wendy, so they decided to build a house around her.

They brought branches and moss for the walls and roof. They used the sole of Tootles's shoe as a door knocker and John's hat as a chimney. When the house was finished, they knocked at the door and waited to see who would answer.

Of course, Wendy answered. She told them she was delighted with her little house, and the lost boys begged her to be their mother.

"But I am just a little girl," she said.

"We just need a kind, motherly person," Peter said.

And so Wendy agreed. She told the boys the story of Cinderella and tucked them in their beds. Later, Peter sat guard outside the door with his sword.

Trees for All

The next day, Peter measured Wendy, John, and Michael for trees. Each lost boy had a hollow tree that fitted him exactly and that he used to go up and down to the underground home. The tree had to be the right size so that no one got stuck or went down too fast. Soon, the newcomers were going up and down easily.

They all loved their underground home. In the middle, a tree tried to grow each day, but they cut it down to use the stump as a table. Tinkerbell had her own alcove with a curtain. Wendy kept busy looking after the boys, mending their socks and doing the cooking, though sometimes the food was only make-believe.

As the weeks passed, Wendy did not worry much about her parents. She was sure they would leave the window open in case she ever returned. She gave John and Michael little quizzes to keep their memories of their parents alive because she was alarmed at how quickly they were forgetting home. In the daytime, they had adventures, or they played at being ordinary boys, tossing a ball to each other.

There were too many adventures to mention them all. One day, the Indians attacked and got stuck in the trees going down to the house. The pirates left the rich cake for the boys as they had planned, but Wendy snatched it away and kept it until it dried out. Then they used pieces of it as missiles to throw at the pirates.

The Mermaid Lagoon

Let's look at just one adventure to get a flavor of life in Neverland.

If you close your eyes really tightly, you might just glimpse the perfect blue of the mermaid lagoon—but that's as close as you will ever get to it on the mainland. The children spent long summer days swimming and floating in the lagoon, but the mermaids were not friendly and dived underwater if the children tried to join their games.

When they played in the lagoon, Wendy insisted that the boys all take a half-hour nap after lunch, lying on Marooners' Rock in the sun. It was a dark place, for evil captains would maroon enemies on the rock and leave them to drown in the rising tide. Still, when the tide was out, it was a good place to rest.

One day, as the boys slept on the rock and Wendy sat stitching, a chill and a shiver fell over the lagoon. "Pirates!" Peter cried, waking from his nap. "Dive!"

They all dived into the lagoon and hid under the water. They dived just in time, for a moment later, a small boat approached the rock. In it, two pirates—Smee and Starkey—held captive the Indian princess Tiger Lily. Hook had found her trying to board a pirate ship. As they approached the rock, Smee said, "Luff, you lubber. Here's the rock and here you'll drown." Wendy started to cry at the tragedy, but Peter had a plan.

Copying Hook's voice, Peter called out, "Ahoy there! Set her free or I'll plunge my hook into you!"

The puzzled pirates did as they thought their captain asked and cut Tiger Lily's ropes. At once, she slid into the water and was gone.

Wendy and Peter then heard, "Boat, ahoy!" in the same voice that Peter had used. Hook was also in the water, swimming toward the rock. Wendy trembled as she watched him haul himself, dripping and fearsome, into the pirate boat.

"The game's up," he sighed. "The lost boys have a mother."

"Perhaps she will help Peter," Starkey said.

"Captain," Smee suggested, "could we capture her and make her our mother?"

"Great scheme!" Hook said. "We'll catch them all, make the boys walk the plank, and make her our mother!"

Wendy, hiding in the water, was horrified.

"Now," Hook went on, "where's the Indian girl?"

"We let her go, as you said," Smee answered.

"Let her go!?" Hook's face was black with rage. "I gave no such order!" He turned his face to the lagoon and called out, "Spirit that haunts the water, do you hear me?"

Peter couldn't resist answering in Hook's voice:

"Odds, bobs, hammer, and tongs, I hear you!"

"Who are you?" Hook called.

"James Hook, captain of the Jolly Roger," Peter answered. Smee and Starkey shook to their boots, but Hook was braver.

"Then who am I?" Hook called.

"A codfish." And so it went on until at last Peter cock-crowed and admitted that he was Peter Pan. All at once, the water was seething with fighting boys and pirates. Hook slashed out with his hook, keeping a clear circle around him.

At last, Hook and Peter found themselves facing each other on Marooners' Rock. Peter snatched a knife from Hook's belt, and Hook bit him. He slashed with his hook—but moments later, Hook was in the water, white with fright and swimming for his life, pursued by the crocodile. Meanwhile, the lost boys took the pirates' boat and went home, calling out over the lagoon to Wendy and Peter, but they could not find them.

Peter and Wendy lay exhausted on Marooners' Rock. The unfriendly mermaids tried to pull Wendy into the water. Peter saved her but had to tell her the truth.

"We're on Marooners' Rock, Wendy. The water is rising and we will be drowned. I am too injured to swim or fly." They covered their eyes and waited to die. But a moment later, Michael's kite floated by. Peter grabbed the string. It would not carry them both but he knew it could carry Wendy. He tied the tail around her and pushed her from the rock.

"Goodbye, Wendy," he called as she rose into the air. He faced the lagoon with a smile, his heart beating fast.

The water rose steadily until it reached his toes. Peter looked out over the lagoon and saw something white floating toward him. He thought that perhaps it was a piece of paper, but it seemed to be fighting the tide. He soon saw it was not paper, but the Never Bird, which makes its nest on the water and floats around until the eggs hatch. The bird called out to Peter, and Peter called to the bird, but neither understood each other. The bird was saying she wanted Peter to get onto the nest, and Peter was saying he didn't understand.

But at last, Peter guessed her intent and pulled the nest toward him as the bird flew into the air. She hung above, watching to see what he would do with her eggs. Peter carefully lifted them from the nest and placed them in Starkey's hat, which was hanging from a pole on the rock. Then he set the hat in the lagoon so that it could float, and he climbed onto the nest. Then he used the pole as a mast and his shirt as a sail, and sailed away. The bird was so pleased with the hat-nest that all Never Birds ever since have built their nests in the shape of a hat with a wide brim for the chicks to stand on.

When at last Peter arrived home, Wendy was already there. All the boys shared their adventures and everyone went to bed much too late!

Wendy's Story

The Piccaninnies were so grateful to Peter for saving Tiger Lily that they now guarded the underground house. The boys ate and slept and bickered, and every night Wendy told them a story. One night, she told her own story. It went like this: Once upon a time, there were two people called Mr. and Mrs. Darling, and they had three children. One night, their children flew off to Neverland, without a thought for the poor parents. Then, long after, when the girl was a woman and her brothers were grown men, they returned home. The window was open and their mother was waiting for them.

"It's not like that," Peter said. "I thought my mother would leave the window open, but when I returned, it was closed and another boy was sleeping in my bed. My mother forgot about me." Who knows if that was true or not, but Peter told it as though it was.

"Let's go home!" John and Michael said together.

"At once!" Wendy said. "Peter, will you help us?"

The lost boys were stricken, but Peter wasn't going to show he cared (even though he cared a lot). He asked the Indians to guide the children. Touched by the lost boys' misery, Wendy said they could all come too, but secretly, it was Peter she really wanted to come. Peter told Tinkerbell to take them all across the sea, which annoyed the fairy greatly. But at that very moment, the pirates launched their attack.

Attack!

The pirate attack was a surprise, so by definition it was unfair. Everyone in Neverland knows that an attack is always started by the Indians; anything else is cheating. The Piccaninnies were horrified, frozen by the shock of the assault. The pirates massacred them, with only Tiger Lily and a few of her guard escaping— though the dead took several pirates with them.

At the first sound of battle, the lost boys stood stock still and waited to see who would win. The noise soon died down. They didn't know it, but the pirates stood above their underground home, wondering how to get their great bulk down the hollow trees. They heard Peter say, "If the Indians have won, they will beat their drum, the tom-tom. It is their sign of victory."

By chance, Smee had found the tom-tom. Hook now signaled to him to beat it. The children below cheered. The pirates waited, one by each tree, for them to come out.

The pirates caught each boy as he came up his tree and tossed him from one to another until they had all the boys in a large pile. When Wendy appeared, Hook took her hand and led her to the pile, while she was too surprised—and perhaps a tiny bit charmed—to object.

The pirates began to tie up all the boys, trussing them like packages with string. All but greedy Slightly, who could not be tied because he bulged out everywhere.

It was clear to Hook that a boy as large as Slightly had become would not have fit through his tree—and it was true that Slightly had whittled away at his tree to make the passage wider. Hook thought at last he had a chance to defeat Peter.

While the pirates carried the bound children to his ship, Hook made his way back to the underground house. He slipped down Slightly's widened tree trunk and stood at last inside the underground house. Peter slept, unknowing, on his bed.

Hook peered into the room. Peter's pose was all cockiness, with a leg raised and an arm flung out, and it prodded Hook to more anger. He gripped his sword, but the low door blocked his way and he could not reach the catch. He shook and rattled the door uselessly. Then he caught sight of Peter's medicine standing within reach on a shelf. Peter had not taken it before sleeping, just because he knew it would annoy Wendy.

Now, Hook always carried a deadly poison of his own invention with him. He dripped five drops of it into Peter's medicine, wriggled back up the tree, and stole away through the trees, sure that Peter was doomed.

Peter woke to a knock at the door. He called out, but no one answered. He said he wouldn't open the door unless they did answer. It was Tinkerbell.

She quickly told Peter about the boys and Wendy being captured on the ship.

"I'll save her!" he cried, grabbing his weapons. And then he thought he'd take his medicine to please Wendy. As he picked it up Tinkerbell cried, "No! It's poisoned!"

"Nonsense!" Peter said. "Who poisoned it?"

Tinkerbell told him it was Hook, but Peter did not believe her. Peter raised the cup to his lips.

Tink darted in and drained the cup herself.

"How dare you?!" Peter cried, furious with Tinkerbell. But she was already falling from the air.

"It was poisoned," she whispered. "Now I will die."

Peter, sobbing, put her into her tiny home.

"Is there anything that can save you?" he asked.

"Maybe if children believed in fairies, I need not die," Tink suggested.

Peter immediately called out to all the dreaming children in the world—for he can do that—to clap their hands if they believed in fairies. Many did. Only a few didn't. Tink's voice grew stronger. Soon, she was flitting around as strong as ever.

"Now to rescue Wendy!" Peter cried.

There was too much light to fly, so he crept through the woods as quietly as a Piccaninny, gripping his dagger and knowing sudden death could be around any corner. Only the crocodile passed him by.

The Pirate Ship

Meanwhile, Hook was sullen and troubled on his ship. Peter was doomed to die from poisoning and he had all the boys captive. His purpose in life was gone.

But he had to deal with the children. He had the pirates bring the boys up on deck.

"Six of you will walk the plank. I have room for two cabin boys," he said. But no one wanted to work for the pirates.

"Then get the plank ready for all of them!" Hook said. "And bring up their mother."

Wendy was brought up, and Hook told her to say her last words to the boys. She was brave and grand:

"Your real mothers would say: 'We hope you will die like gentlemen.'"

Hook commanded Smee to tie her to the mast to watch. The boys shivered as they looked at the plank—that last, short walk they would soon take.

At that moment, they all heard: tick tick tick tick.

It was the crocodile! Hook collapsed to the deck as if every joint in his body had been snipped. Then he crawled to the back of the ship and told his pirates to hide him. The boys wriggled free and ran to look over the edge to where the crocodile was boarding the ship.

But they saw no crocodile. What they saw was Peter Pan, who signaled to them to keep the secret, while he carried on ticking.

As Peter was stealing through the forest, the crocodile passed him and he noticed she wasn't ticking. So he started to tick himself to keep the other wild beasts away. He had not intended to trick Hook, but now he realized what a good idea it had been.

No sooner was Peter on board, than a pirate came to investigate. Peter stabbed him with his dagger and threw him overboard.

"One!" counted Slightly.

Peter slipped into the cabin to hide from the pirates. He'd stopped ticking now and Hook felt braver, assured by his men that the crocodile had gone. He set about making the boys walk the plank and sent Jukes to fetch the cat-o'-nine-tails from the cabin. The boys quaked as they all waited, but instead of Jukes coming from the cabin, there came a terrible screech and then a cock-a-doodle-doo. The boys knew what that meant.

Hook sent Pirate Cecco to look in the cabin.

"Jukes is dead," Cecco said. "The cabin's as black as a pit and something terrible is in there."

"Two," muttered Slightly.

"Fetch that cock-a-doodle," Hook demanded.

Cecco went. Again a scream and the crowing.

"Three," Slightly whispered.

Next it was Starkey, but he would mutiny rather than go into the cabin, and leaped into the sea.

"Four," Slightly said.

Hook seized a lantern.

"I'll do it myself!" he grumbled, going into the cabin.

He staggered out a moment later, his lantern dark.

"Something blew out the light," he said, a lot less brave than he had been. "Lads, let's push all the boys in there. They can deal with it or it can deal with them!"

They shoved the boys into the cabin, locked the door and waited, listening. Inside, Peter unlocked the boys' chains. Then he went to find Wendy. He wrapped himself in Wendy's cloak, crowed loudly, and took her place at the mast. While this was going on, the pirates debated what to do.

"It's bad luck to have a girl on board. Let's fling her overboard!"

Hook approached the mast.

"No one can save you now!" he said.

"One can—Peter Pan!" Peter said, flinging off the cloak.

"Cleave him to the brisket!" shouted Hook, and the boys and pirates fell upon each other.

If the pirates had been well prepared, they would have won, but they were scattered and disorganized. Some jumped into the sea and others tried to hide, but Slightly led the other boys to them. Swords clashed and the air rang with screams and splashes. Again and again the boys surrounded Hook, but he drove them back. He was impossible to defeat. At last, Peter sprang before him.

"Keep back," he said to his boys, "this man is mine."

The Final Battle

"So," Hook said, "This is all your doing? Proud, insolent youth, prepare to meet your doom."

"Prepare to die, dark and sinister man," Peter responded. Then they fell to the battle, with thrusts and lunges and slashes and swipes, until Peter cut Hook's hand and he dropped his sword.

"Now!" cried the lost boys, but Peter let Hook pick up his sword and begin again. Confounded by Peter's good manners, Hook flailed wildly while Peter was nimble and quick, pricking again and again at the pirate. At last, Hook set light to the gunpowder box.

"The ship will blow up!" he cried. But Peter threw the box overboard. Now Hook's fighting was ragged, and soon Peter had forced him to the end of the ship. Hook jumped onto the edge, ready to plunge into the sea as Peter approached with his dagger, but at the last moment, Peter kicked him, and over he went, down into the sea— into the jaws of the waiting crocodile. That was the end of Captain Hook.

"Seventeen!" Slightly sang out.

It was one thirty in the morning. Wendy rushed the boys into bed in the pirates' hammocks. Going to bed so late was almost the most exciting part.

The next day, with Peter as captain, the ship set off for the mainland. They sailed as far as the Azores, and then Peter said it would be quicker to fly.

Home Again

Let's return now to the home the children left behind. Mr. Darling had vowed to stay in the kennel until the children returned, because they would never have been lost if he had not banished Nana. One Thursday, Mrs. Darling was dozing in the day nursery. When Mr. Darling came home, he asked her to play the piano until he slept and to close the window against the draft.

"You know I will not close the window!" she replied, but she went into the next room to the piano. As Mr. Darling slept in the night nursery, Peter Pan and Tinkerbell flew in.

"Quick, Tink, close the window," Peter said. He flew around, watching Mrs. Darling play the piano and cry.

"You want me to undo the window," he said (though she couldn't hear him), "but I won't. I'm fond of her, too; we can't both have her."

But the Darlings' sorrow was too much to bear. At last, he told Tinkerbell to open the window.

"We don't need any silly mothers!" he said, flying out.

So when Wendy and John and Michael arrived, the window was open. The boys barely recognized their old house, but they slipped into their beds and looked as though they had never been away.

Mrs. Darling saw the occupied beds, but she did not really believe her children were there until they leaped up and ran to her. Then father and Nana saw them, too, and no family could have been happier.

As for the lost boys, although Mr. Darling thought six would be quite a handful, they all managed to fit in and were not too much trouble after all. But Peter would not stay because Mrs. Darling said he would have to go to school and grow into a man.

You would think that was the end of the story, but Peter promised to collect Wendy for one week every year to help with spring cleaning. But he forgot more often than he came. Then one year when he came, Wendy was grown up with a daughter of her own named Jane.

At first, Wendy shrank down in her chair, afraid to let Peter see she had grown up. But she had to tell him, and revealed the sleeping child was her daughter.

"It's not true!" sobbed Peter. "You promised you wouldn't grow up!" Wendy didn't know what to do, and ran from the room. Jane woke up.

"Boy," she said, "why are you crying?"

He bowed to her. "I am Peter Pan," he said.

But Jane knew that already. Soon, Peter had her flying around the room. Wendy came in just as they reached the window.

"Just for spring cleaning," Jane pleaded. At last, Wendy let her go for a week, each year that Peter remembered. And later, Jane's daughter, Margaret, went with Peter Pan. And when she is grown up, her daughter will go, and so it will go on, for as long as children are cheery and innocent and unthinking.

About the Author

Sir James Matthew Barrie was born in Scotland in 1860. Barrie worked as a journalist before writing a series of popular novels. In the 1890s he turned to writing plays, and during long walks in Kensington Gardens in London, he met the Davies family. The five brothers of the family provided the inspiration for his most famous work—*Peter Pan*. Barrie even named three of the characters after the brothers—Michael, John, and Peter. First performed as a play in 1904, *Peter Pan* was made into a book in 1911 and has since been reproduced as a pantomime, a musical, and as several films.

Other titles in the *Illustrated Classics* series:
The Adventures of King Arthur and His Knights • *The Adventures of Tom Sawyer*
• *Alice's Adventures in Wonderland* • *Anne of Green Gables* • *Black Beauty* • *Greek Myths*
• *Gulliver's Travels* • *Heidi* • *A Little Princess* • *Little Women* • *Pinocchio* • *Robin Hood*
• *Robinson Crusoe* • *The Secret Garden* • *Sherlock Holmes* • *The Swiss Family Robinson*
• *The Three Musketeers* • *Treasure Island* • *White Fang* • *The Wizard of Oz*
• *20,000 Leagues Under The Sea*

An Imprint of Sterling Publishing
387 Park Avenue South
New York, NY 10016

Text © 2015 by QEB Publishing, Inc.
Illustrations © 2015 by QEB Publishing, Inc.

This 2015 edition published by Sandy Creek.

ISBN 978-1-4351-5824-5

Editorial Director: Victoria Garrard • Designers: Rachel Clark and Rachel Lawston • Art Director: Laura Roberts-Jensen

Manufactured in Guangdong, China
Lot #:
10 9 8 7 6 5 4 3 2 1
01/15